# PREPARING FOR A CROWN

A Bible Study for Teens
and Young Women

MELINDA CULP

WESTBOW°
PRESS
A DIVISION OF THOMAS NELSON
& ZONDERVAN

Scripture taken from the Holy Bible, NEW INTERNATIONAL VERSION®.
Copyright © 1973, 1978, 1984 by Biblica, Inc. All rights reserved worldwide.
Used by permission. NEW INTERNATIONAL VERSION® and NIV® are
registered trademarks of Biblica, Inc. Use of either trademark for the offering
of goods or services requires the prior written consent of Biblica US, Inc.

WestBow Press books may be ordered through booksellers or by contacting:

WestBow Press
A Division of Thomas Nelson & Zondervan
1663 Liberty Drive
Bloomington, IN 47403
www.westbowpress.com
1 (866) 928-1240

Because of the dynamic nature of the Internet, any web addresses or
links contained in this book may have changed since publication and
may no longer be valid. The views expressed in this work are solely those
of the author and do not necessarily reflect the views of the publisher,
and the publisher hereby disclaims any responsibility for them.

Any people depicted in stock imagery provided by Thinkstock are models,
and such images are being used for illustrative purposes only.
Certain stock imagery © Thinkstock.

ISBN: 978-1-4908-7644-3 (sc)

Library of Congress Control Number: 2015905682

Print information available on the last page.

WestBow Press rev. date: 4/21/2015

I would like to thank my wonderful husband, Shane, for his continued support, encouragement and prayer during this process. He has been wonderful to join me in prayer to ensure that God's message was clear to me.

I would also like to thank Mrs. Barbara Stecklein for her time and efforts for using up her red pens on my drafts.

# CONTENTS

A FEW YEARS AGO GOD gave me the opportunity to speak to a group of ladies at a women's retreat. This then led to other local opportunities for me and then to even have a routine meeting of ladies held at the church my husband was pastoring. The more I was able to serve; the more I knew that God was calling me to spend my ministry with women. I was particularly drawn to work with young women as I had lots of great examples for them.

I grew up in a Christian home and was taught all the right things and was shown on a daily basis how to serve others. I, however, decided to run away from the lifestyle that I was taught and believed in while in high school and then into my college career. I had decided that I knew enough to stay out of trouble, have fun and still be a "good" girl. All I did was get farther and farther from God and the truth. I would attend church routinely with my college roommate and play the game, but my heart was very heavy. I knew that something was missing in my life. I tried to fill the void with many things but the void grew darker and deeper. The void was able to get rid of the joy that I once had in my life and the desires that I had and the love to serve others.

I was able to overcome the void I had allowed to come into my life and once again focus on the God that created me and to form that relationship again with Him. I, like many young women, know what we are to say, the way we are to behave and where we are suppose to be. But ladies, Satan is real! He knows how to get into our minds when we are the most vulnerable and lead us astray while we are thinking that we are still doing what we are supposed to. I let my guard down, and Satan took the opportunity to get me farther and farther from my relationship with God. I was trying to be someone that I was not, and in doing so lost many friends and did a lot of damage to many relationships that I had with others.

Many young women go through what I have. Some find their way back into their relationship with God, and some do not. They believe the lies that Satan has given us: that we no longer are good enough and we can not be forgiven for what we have done. I beg to differ though. God tells His people in the Old Testament and again in the New "Never will I leave you; never will I forsake you" Hebrews 13:5. God has not left us; we have done the leaving. God is the one constant that we have in our lives. We can not expect the constant to be a friend, a thing, or a relationship that we have with some person. We are all sinners and things will not last. "Jesus Christ is the same yesterday and today and forever" Hebrews 13:8. What great reassurance that He is the constant in our lives. It is easier said than done to keep that relationship with Him.

Even now I strive to have the relationship with God that I know and desire to have, but I still mess up. I still allow the things of this world and life to fill up my day and get too busy! I still try to make decisions on my own without seeking God's will. I drive an hour and a half to get to work each morning, and I focus that time to spend in prayer and worship so I can start the day off right. I do well for a while, but then I let other things get in the way of what I worked so hard to for in the morning. God knows the desires of our hearts. Do you know the desire of your own heart?

In many of the Bible studies that I was asked to do for women, God kept taking me back to the passage of Esther. I know that we all know the story of Esther: a common girl taken to the palace, the king loved her, she became queen, and she saved the Jews from death. Good story! But there is so much more that we can learn from Esther. Each of the Bible studies had a different take and was from a different period during Esther's time. The richness of the details can be applied to many of our lives and the different seasons of our lives.

Esther's story truly begins around 732 B.C. in 2 Kings 17: 7-23. This is where the Tribe of Benjamin was exiled from Jerusalem by King Nebuchadnezzar. During their exile many of the Israelites settled among cities of the Medes and began obtaining positions of importance and wealth in the cities. This is a long shot from the slaves that they had been in the past! The Jews were once again sinning against God, since the time that they had been brought out of slavery in Egypt. This was a terrible pattern that they kept getting into (one that we stay in ourselves). They were worshiping other gods and participating in other ungodly acts (AGAIN!), and God has once again warned them.

So thanks to the exile of her ancestors, Esther is in Susa. Her Jewish name is Hadassah which means "lovely in form." She is being raised by her cousin because both of her parents had died. Her journey from orphan to queen to hero is where we are going to dig. Not all of the sections my apply to you at this point in your life; you may have already gone through this season and either conquered it or you are trying to suppress that time. If you were able to conquer it, then please take time to give God the glory and praise for where you were and where you are now. If you have suppressed that time, please stop and ask God to show you something new through this study. Allow God to work through His word in the story of Esther and show you how you can still be forgiven and be able to continue on. Maybe you need to forgive someone else before you can move on.

I am not saying that any of the feelings that you are going to come up against or hurt that you have experienced is going to go away. On the contrary, the thoughts and emotions will probably still be there; however, the burden that you carry around because of decisions can be removed, and eventually you will be able to share your story and give God the glory for the removal of the shackles in your life. God is "not ashamed of my chains He will show mercy to us" 2 Timothy 1:16. Allow God to show you the chains that are still holding you back and then allow Him to break those chains and set you free.

We are going to start by looking into the relationship that we may have with men. There are two main characters that we are going to look at in Esther: King Xerses(the bad guy) and Mordecia (the good guy). I always liked the "bad guys" growing up because it drove my parents insane! I did end up with a good guy but that was no easy task! As we discuss the relationship style with each one, try to examine your own relationships to see if they fall within either on of these examples.

My dear sister, I am very excited to start this with you! My prayer is that you will develop a closer relationship with God and that you will be truthful with yourself. I have worked with several groups of women through many Bible studies and you many not want to share any of this with anyone else. The truth may still hurt. Just remember to keep sharing with God. Be open with Him. Remember, He already knows your heart, your thoughts, behaviors, and actions. It will be less painful to be open and share with Him.

# THE BAD BOYS:
# XERXES

IN ESTHER, XERXES IS, OF course, the king of Persia. So one might think that it would be a prize to marry the king. However, Xerxes shows several flaws that as young women we should be looking out for in the young men that we choose. From reading Esther, one can come to the conclusion that King Xerxes was not a believer of God. Not only is God never mentioned, but also King Xerxes looks to men for all his answers, never to God. Jesus tells us over and over that the only truth will come from Him. John 14:6 says "Jesus answered, "I am the way and the truth and the life. No one comes to the Father except through me." He also told us "And I will ask the Father and he will give you another Counselor to be with you forever- the Spirit of truth. The world cannot accept him, because it neither sees him nor knows him. But you know him, for he lives with you and will be in you." John 14: 16-17.

You are going to find many people that believe God exist, but it is very difficult to find those that believe "in" God. I am sure that you have seen men together; they can be worse than a group of women together. I am learning this the more I am around them. As much as they are not going to admit it to you and me, they, like us, value the opinion of their male counterparts. They want the acceptance of the men that they are friends with.

We do not need to seek the counsel of all those around us when a decision is needing to be made. We can go straight to the feet of God. The one thing that gets everyone in a frenzy is the fact that you may not hear an answer at that very moment. Many people have a hard time being still so they can hear God. God speaks in a very still small voice (I Kings 19:11-13) To truly hear God we have to stop and listen for Him. God is much easier to talk to than our friends or family. I have found that I can start just rattling off all my thoughts to Him. Granted, He already know what counsel I am seeking from Him, but He is not going to judge me, tell someone else about our conversation, or have weird reactions to what I am telling Him.

You do not want to be in a relationship where you are trusting the male and after you start to confide in him, the next thing you know, all the men that he plays ball with know your deep, dark secrets. A lot can be said for the man that can hold his tongue. King Xerxes was not one to hold his tongue. You can also imagine that after seven days of alcoholic beverage his tongue was quite loose. There is no telling what information he has shared regarding Queen Vashti and/or the harem. The loose tongue of another can cut through you faster than your own tongue can do damage to your moral. A relationship that you are having with another must have trust! Many of your "bad boys" are not going to have those trust characteristics, and you are just a new prize to tell everyone about.

Xerxes also liked to brag and show off what he had. He never once gave credit to God for what he had. The book of Esther starts out with Xerxes throwing a banquet. This banquet was for everyone, and nothing was held back. Xerxes brought out the best of everything that they had, including the garden hangings, the couches, the goblets and the best wine (1: 6-8). He did not stop there. He also wanted to show off his queen and allow everyone to see just how beautiful she was (1:11). Not only did he want to show her off, he was doing this at a time that everyone had been drinking for seven days. Now we all know what wine will do to people. But once you have been partying for seven days, can you imagine the cat calls that Queen Vashti might have received at that time. There would have been no tongue held back at that time.

We all like for our friends, boyfriends or spouses to show us off at times. We want them to be proud of us, but there is a huge difference in someone being proud of us and someone showing us off as a possession. There are women who have never had the experience of someone being proud of them. To their partner they are a piece of meat and a possession. You may be one of these women. It is easy to fall into this category, but dear sister, you can get out of it! You are someone that you and others can be proud of. Keep reading, we will make changes together.

King Xerxes was displaying pride in everything he owned and everything that he thought he owned. The Bible gives us several warnings regarding pride: Proverbs 13:10 tells us that "pride only breeds quarrels," King Xerxes' pride bought him a quarrel with his bride. They were not seeing eye to eye on her parading in front of the men of Susa. Instead of having an adult discussion regarding this disagreement, King Xerxes sought the wisdom of men and then decided what was to be done with Queen Vashti. Proverbs 29:23 "A man's pride brings him low." Once Queen Vashti turned King Xerxes down, he was going to make an example out of her. So he then bans her and issues a decree that all women are to obey their husbands. Now, women are instructed to "submit to their husbands" (Ephesians 5:22), but I do not think that this was the obey that King Xerxes had in mind. There is a vast difference in a women submitting to her spouse and being demanded and expected to obey. To submit to your spouse, you are doing so out of love and respect for him and his position in your family, as your partner. To be demanded to do something makes a women very bitter, withdrawn, angry and many more very negative emotions. There is NO JOY in a relationship that is demanding you to obey your spouse.

King Xerxes allowed anger to affect his emotions and make rash decisions. In Esther 1:12 it lets us know that he was "furious and burned with anger." Anger is a very strong emotion. Think of a situation that made you mad; how did you react? Now think of a situation that made you angry; how did you react? Is there a difference? Absolutely! When we are angry, it truly does burn within us. When we are angry, we react to the situation without thinking clearly. Our emotions drive all of our decision making processes, therefore, leading to sin in our lives. We can allow anger to build and fester if it is not dealt with. Anger is not healthy for anyone to have in his or her life. Ephesians 4:26-27 "In your anger do not sin. Do not let the sun go down while you are still angry, and do not give the devil a foothold." Why would the devil get a foothold? The more you think about the situation or someone that has made you angry, the more you plot at ways to get even with that person. You want to see something bad happen to them. You want them to get caught. You can not tell me you have not done this. I do it in the car! Someone is cutting people off in traffic and driving recklessly; I hope for a cop to be watching. . .this may seam like a minor example, but it is doing the same thing. You cut me off. . .now you get a ticket. . . you deserve it.

We now come to a very important part of King Xerxes decision process. He did not choose either wife for love, but for beauty. I don't know about you, but there is a lot more to me than what you see. God has a very special spouse for each of us. (A spouse of the opposite sex I must include.) You cannot tell me that King Xerxes was in his relationship with Queen Vashti for love when he was demanding her to parade in front of others and then he was willing to throw her out like a soiled towel. When you are in love with your spouse, you want to protect him, to do what is in his best interest and not place them in a compromising position. Love takes a lot of work from both the husband and the wife. Xeres' nobles were trying to end the "disrespect and discord" by issuing an edict, but they did not realize that an edict was not necessary. If the respect towards your spouse would occur; it would be reciprocated.

Also remember that Esther was not jumping up and down at the chance to be chosen by the king. My Bible says that Esther was "taken to the king's palace and entrusted to Hegai." (2:8) She also had to "hide" her true identity. She partook of food and portions that she did not believe in taking, she was being called Esther instead of her Jewish name Hadassah, and when she heard the edict she tried to hide everything about her identity again. Many times if we are around others that are not Christians we suppress our identity. For many reasons we keep our secrets: pride, embarrassment, we want to be like everyone else and fit in, your list can go on and on depending on those that you are with. The more that suppresses our true identity, the more we believe the other one that we are taking on. We grow farther from the truth and sink more into the lies and work harder to keep the lie going. These lies will end up binding us like chains. We become a prisoner of our own creation. It is only through the grace of God that our chains can be removed.

Growing up I hung out around the police department (because it was next to my dad's office), and the dispatcher would chase my brother and me around and put us in handcuffs for fun. The more I wiggled and wrestled with those cuffs the tighter they became. Once they were removed an indention was left, along with the tingling in my hands. Just like our chains that we create with our lies, their indention is left in our lives forever. You may always have the tingling and scars to remind you of your decisions, or you may have been bound too long and have become numb to their effect. What is the best way to overcome these pains? PREVENTION! Don't get caught up with the lies and the trouble to begin with. Start by staying who you are; do not take on another identity just to fit in or to get the guy. You will flourish when you are who God has made you to be. He created you in His image, His perfect image. Why try to recreate yourself out of something that is not perfect and born into sin?

You may be thinking that you are not choosing the "bad" guys. You know as a good little Christian girl which guys to choose, but that is easier said than done. Kudos to you if you are choosing the right Christian boys every time and being chaperoned while you are on your outings. I was not that good. I knew everything that I was supposed to do, but my pride, my rebellion and my needing to prove I could make my own decisions got in the way of my good decision making process.

While I was in high school, I thought that I should "show" my parents that I could make my own decisions in spite of their opinions and make their lives miserable. I willfully made many decisions that I knew weren't in my best interest. My daddy would always do a background check on the guys that I would "date" in high school. Knowing that he performed his check, I decided to seek out the boys that I knew already had a record. You would think that if someone already had a record prior to his 18th birthday that should be a huge red flag to the good little Christian girl I was suppose to be.

Getting caught up in my game, I became entrapped by the sins that I was associated with. Just because I was not actively participating in the activities that these young men, (whether it was drugs, alcohol, sex, smoking, etc.) I was in the company of those participating; therefore I was GUILTY. The next thing you know, I was trying to hide the activities and the places I had been. In case you had not noticed before, smells actually do linger on your clothes; Febreeze and perfume are not cover alls.

It started getting easier and easier to find young men with a rap sheet, in doing so I got a reputation for hanging out with a particular group of people. Whether participated in all the activities or not, I was labeled. Thanks to my trying to "show" my parents, I lost my good friends, my reputation, and the fun that I once had. I ended up spending the majority of my senior year in high school grounded from every extra activity I wanted to do. I went to the ball field, to school and home. My parents even prepared to send me to military school. Having all the brochures laid out on the kitchen table with the requirements and rules was finally a show stopper. All I had to do for my parents to not send me away was to give up the guys that I had sought out to hurt others. That was actually an easy decision.

You see, I was miserable, lonely and tired of feeling alone and used. It has taken years to repair the damage to relationships with many of my once best friends. Your best friends can only take so much hurt themselves before they are going to remove themselves from a bad situation. It took years of the Holy Spirit speaking to me and breaking my heart for me to finally send my long lost best friend a letter apologizing for the ways that I had treated her so wrongly, for not being there when she was going through very tough times in her life. I had ended up letting her down on many levels. The very things that we promised we would never do to each other, I did them. . . I did them ALL. But with the Holy Spirit working in me, and finally accepting what I was being told to do, I learned that the past that had been haunting me, had been forgiven years ago. We now have a relationship again, not near like the one we had while in junior high and high school, but a relationship.

The wrong guy can really lead to your down fall, as you can see. By the time I graduated from high school and was heading to college, I had learned my lesson. I was moving out of state to Arkansas and was focusing on my education and career. I was going to make a name for myself. And then it happened. The summer between high school and college I met a young man. Yes, I know, I was done with boys. I have a dependency issue with them. I was determined that I was only going to date him and have fun. You see there are lots of fish in the sea when you are in college right? But I was falling fast for this one. So, I did what every responsible young Christian girl would do, I asked him if he knew Jesus. He said YES! I had hit the jack pot! I actually found a good guy; he would go to church with me when he would visit me in Arkansas, and he knew Jesus. Life was good! After only knowing him for about 1 ½ years we said "I do." Things were good for awhile, but then I learned that I had not asked the right question. Yes, he knew who Jesus was, but Jesus was not his Lord and Savior.

So did this question matter? Absolutely. We were on two different pages. I had read several times in the Bible about being unequally yoked; this scripture suddenly had more meaning for me than it ever had before. I tried going to church a few times with him, but I received all the excuses in the book. He was good at them, and I was beginning to feel guilty. I was not spending time with him, I did not get home soon enough, it was throwing the whole day off. You name it, I heard it. I once again found myself miserable.

I do not believe in divorce; now I know that there are circumstances that happen where it is best for all involved, especially when there is abuse involved. However, I was not about to let people know that I had been defeated, that anyone else was right, or that I was giving up. (I was a little hard headed back in the day). You want to talk about some serious prayer, I was there. That was the first time in my life that I poured my heart out to the Lord. I was broken, and the desires of my heart were laid at His feet. While the tears would flow, I would let God know of the mistakes that I had made.

I thought that I had done what I was suppose to do. I but had not sought out God's ways for me to handle my life decisions, or any decisions for that matter. I was using the training that I had received, but I was not going directly to the Teacher for the one on one tutoring. Praise God that through many prayers and being totally broken, my husband accepted Jesus into his heart as his personal Lord and Savior and has been following God's plan for us since.

Please note that we are the exception to this story. Many young women have gone through circumstances like mine. However, their stories do not always end well. Many are beaten emotionally and/or physically. Many are pulled away from God and are filling the gap with things, substances, you fill in the blank, and not being satisfied. You see, we are all born with a hole in our lives that needs filled. This is a God size hole and nothing will fit in it except for God. Nothing in this world can take His place or do the great and mighty things that only He can do. So no matter what you try to place in His spot, it will not fit. There is always room for more junk.

Do you remember the toy that toddlers have that is a big ball with different shaped holes cut in it? You then have the different shapes that the toddler is to match up with the hole to place it in the ball. Well, some of the shapes are smaller than others. At times you could maneuver the circle into the square, but it was not a perfect fit. You still had all the corners unfilled. So you then try to cram some other shape into the square also. This is what we do with all the junk we try to fill in God's hole. You will never find the perfect fit until God is placed in it.

# Self Evaluation

Am I choosing the "bad" boys to date? Why is it that this is the type of young man I am wanting to hang around?

Does the young man or others in the past have characteristics of King Xerxes? Are they displaying me for bragging rights, letting pride take over, easily angered, and only with me because of my appearance?

Has my relationship labeled me? What kind of label is it? How do I overcome the label that I have.

Do I want to be in a relationship that I am constantly emotionally or physically hurt?

Is the love for my future spouse that God has designed important enough to learn about and fight for?

Am I in a relationship now that I should not be in? Who can I turn to that will help me and pray with me to get out safely?

Do I believe I am special enough to have pride in who I am and I am ready to not allow others and my relationship with them define me poorly? Read Psalm 139.

Identify in Psalm 139 why I am so special and unique. I praise You God now because. . . . .

# MORDECAI
# (THE GOOD GUYS)

M ORDECAI IS ACTUALLY THE COUSIN of Esther. Not only is he her cousin, but he was raising her as his daughter. Esther's parents had both died, so she was an orphan. Mordecai demonstrates several characteristics that as women we should be seeking out. Now I know that that King Xerxes and the others can be attractive because they tend to have a "bad" boy trait to them; however, the good guys can have a "wild" and strong streak to them that is even more appealing. I also know that Mordecai is not the perfect man. If you are looking for one, you can only find one. That man is Jesus Christ. He is the only one to walk a sinless life. Even though we can not find a man that is perfect, we can definitely have high standards in the young men we want to hang around. There are some that are trying to live the life that God has called them to have. Don't give up quickly and become frustrated. Just as you are trying to figure out how to be the young woman that God has called you to be and trying to understand what company to keep, they are facing similar struggles.

Mordecai starts out by demonstrating a caring and responsible attribute by caring for Esther when she was left alone once her parents had died. Mordecai could have allowed her to be sold into slavery or prostitution when her parents died because Esther 2:7 lets us know that Esther was lovely in form and features; this could have brought a lot of money and favor to Mordecai. Instead, he treated her like his own daughter. It says a great deal about a man who is willing to actually care for someone else. To put his own needs aside and tend to the needs of someone else shows servanthood. It is hard to be a servant to others, putting them first. We are very selfish beings and like to have ourselves taken care of first. There are many days that after working all day, fixing dinner and cleaning the kitchen that I just want time to myself. I want to sit back and wallow in my own self-pity for the day. Everyone can wait on me right? God did not create us to sit around and be waited on, especially when we are physically and mentally capable of helping others.

When Jesus came to the earth, He served those around Him, to the point of washing others' feet. We can be called to service at any time. Luke 12: 35 says "Be dressed ready for service keep your lamps burning." It may not be that someone has passed and you are needing to take in a family member, but someone may be ill, need tutoring, or need you to come and stand by them while they are trying to accomplish something that is scary for them (speech, volunteering, etc). If you are too busy tending to your own "needs" and ignoring the needs of others, you are going to miss your opportunity to serve. Mordecai easily could have refused to take Esther; but because he was willing, the Jews were not annihilated. Do you prefer to be around people that are only thinking of themselves? No, because your opinion is never important to them and you are probably doing all the work; leaving you miserable and tired.

There are several examples in the Bible of being a servant. One in particular regarding Mary and Martha comes to mind. In Luke 10:38-42 Jesus goes to the home of Mary and Martha. Martha had busied herself making preparations while her sister sat at the feet of Jesus. Jesus tells Martha to basically leave Mary alone, her decision was a wise one, and she has come to sit at his feet listen to him. Martha is not busy "serving others." She is making a production of Jesus coming into her home. You may remember that the next time Jesus comes to visit, it is Mary again who sits at his feet and takes perfume and washes his feet with the perfume and her hair. Mary is the one being a true servant.

I can relate to this very well. I live with my husband and 2 small boys (3 boys in total). When I know that company is coming, I go crazy and I want the house clean. My house is never clean with those three, but I expect it to be when others come by. So, the night before the company is to arrive, I stay up late and start to scrub. I become like Jekel and Hyde throwing things away, griping about what they have and haven't done, and doing laundry. The next day I then get up early to make sure they do not mess the house up again and to fix a very grand meal for all to partake of. In doing so, I completely miss out on the enjoyment of my company. I am too exhausted to enjoy myself or the time to visit with them. All I can think about is what part of the house I forgot to clean and getting the kitchen cleaned up when they are gone. People do not care how sparkling clean my house is or how elaborate my cooking skills are. What is important is the time that I take with them while they are in my company and how I served them while they were there.

Mordecai also was a servant to Esther when she was taken into the palace, he did not leave her on her own. He checked on her everyday and encouraged her to keep her identity safe. He was dedicated to her. He could have easily jumped for joy that he was rid of her; he no longer had to clothe, feed, or give her shelter. The palace was now taking care of all of these things. Instead, he went to the palace every day to check on her (Esther 2:11). There had to be some sense of uncertainty, confusion and even timidness on Esther's part once she was taken to the harem. To know that someone loved her enough to daily take time out of his schedule to check on her and see how she was doing surely gave Esther a little bit of hope. There are many times that we are put into situations or places that we feel out of place or uncomfortable with the setting and company; however, if there is a familiar face that we see, the situation can perk up for us. We are encouraged by the presence of others we trust. As Christians we are to "therefore encourage one another and build each other up. . ." I Thessalonians 5:11, this is not just towards other Christians, but in all our relationships.

There are several times that I have come home from a day at work that has me worn down, but encouraging words from my spouse have lifted me up very quickly. Words have a lot of power to them. It is important to know that the words that are spoken to you from a man that you are in a relationship with will hurt or lift you up more than anyone else's words. Someone at work can tell me that I messed up and critique me and I can move on, but if my spouse tells me that I messed up and critiques me, I am a basket case because I have disappointed him. Many young women today are trapped in relationships. They are tied by the horrible words that are told to them on a daily basis. Those words get inside their mind and Satan takes them and begins to stretch them like silly putty. The more it is stretched, the stickier it becomes, and you can not get it all back together and put up. Once Satan is able to get those horrible words in a person's mind, he stretches them and they become stuck and then they multiply, never going away until they are stuck for good and the person believes them. Do not get yourself into a relationship that is a war game; you will not win. Mordecai may not have been able to speak to Esther, but his presence was enough. Young men that will take a back seat and encourage you are rare, I know, but they are out there. Don't just settle on one thinking they will grow out of being non-encouraging, because they will not, it will only get worse. "Reckless words pierce like a sword, but the tongue of the wise brings healing." Proverbs 12: 18

Mordecai stood firm in his beliefs, he knew better than to bow down to anyone than the one true God. Mordecai could have easily bowed down to Haman like the others, but where would that have placed God in his life? The ten commandments clearly tell us, we are to place no one and nothing above God. Deuteronomy 5:9 says, "You shall not bow down to them or worship them; for I, the Lord your God, am a jealous God. . ." So you stopped there and said the commandments are talking about idols. Remember, what is an idol? Anything that has taken the place of God in your life is to be considered an idol. Ouch! That could be a boy, a television show, phones, sports, money, the list could go on and on. We get so tied up with our things and people that God is placed in the back of our minds, and when that happens, we have brought an idol into our life. Even though the King had elevated Haman above all the other nobles and, therefore, people were to bow to him to pay him honor (3:2).

It is not easy to stand firm in your beliefs. Mordecai stood firm, and for that Haman was going to see to it that he and all the Jews were punished. Mordecai could have very easily complied with the request to bow at the feet of Haman; he was questioned several times as to why he would not, but he did not break. You may not be asked to bow at someone's feet, but how many times are you giving into the pressures around you that you know you should not be participating in? The activity(s) are not pleasing to God, but you are doing them anyway to prevent the insults that might be sent your way or because you would be rejected by people if you did not. We say that we will stand firm, but the first time we are at that party and are asked to participate in an activity (drugs, alcohol, sex, pornography, etc) we often give in. Having a guy like Mordecai around, who is also willing to stand firm, will help you stand firm. It may/could actually prevent you from many being in many of those circumstances to begin with.

As a Christian you will be persecuted for the decisions that you are making if you are following Christ. We actually were speaking today in Sunday School Class about an article that had been in the local newspaper. The author of the article pointed out that the persecution of Christians was occurring all around us, not to the extreme that those in other countries were witnessing, but to a new level of bullying, making fun of, and isolating us. Godly choices are not always the popular choices, but "blessed are those who are persecuted because of righteousness, for theirs is the kingdom of heaven." Matthew 5:10.

Mordecai was a man that was not afraid to show his emotions. Yes, I know that his existence was about to end, and I would be a little emotional also, but it did not stop him from bawling like a baby. You many not think that it is important for a man to show his emotional side, but it is. As a woman I like to have a softer side at times, which could be surprising to some. In my spare time I like to watch movies on the Hallmark and the Disney channels. Why? Because they tend to show more emotions, the touchy feely type of emotions, and I can cry through them all. These movies by the end tend to show the softer side of the man. They are romantic and willing to cry and tell the girl how much they really love them. Then I can sit around and wonder and even get mad sometimes that my husband does not do those things for me. As a woman you need to experience the softer side. You need to know that he is not as cold as ice and hard as a rock. It is important for us to be able to share our true feelings with those around us. To be able to let him know in a loving way when he has hurt us does a lot for our emotions and the other person involved. If you are not able to share your feelings and vice versa with him, many times you will end up with a false sense of what is really going on between the two of you when troubles arise.

Like I said before, you are not going to be able to find a guy that is "perfect," but the perfect guy for you is out there. God has created someone for all of us. Remember God started off by creating man and said that he needed a helpmate, a woman. That is right; they need us just as much as we need them. Remember, you don't have to rush into anything. Take your time, study God's word, and determine the type of man that God wants you to have a relationship with. You may end up learning more about yourself than you do some boy!

# Self Evaluation

Do I understand what it means to submit to another?

Am I too demanding and overbearing that I have not been displaying characteristics of caring and responsible person?

Am I ready to be a servant to those around me, or I am always placing myself in a position for others to serve me?

Do I use words towards others that are encouraging or are they demeaning? How do I make sure that I am using encouraging words?

Have I been allowing myself to seek out a relationship that we could work out together?

How do I plan on a relationship growing as two becoming one.

Am I putting "labels" on men that have a softer side and are not the "bad boys" because they are not participating in activities that they should not be in?

Read I Timothy 6:3-21. These are things that Timothy was charged to have, characteristics that he should take on in his life.

Which of these characteristics are important to you?

Do you feel that you should be more important to someone than his things?

Should you be cherished and worth the fight?

Take the opportunity to pray for God to give you the knowledge and understanding of what it means to be a helpmate in the relationship that he has for you. Ask Him to start preparing you and your mate (or future mate) for a lifetime of love/joy/trials/etc. Thank God for the God fearing men that are in your life now.

# ESTHER (WINNING THE FAVOR OF OTHERS)

A FTER ESTHER WAS TAKEN TO the palace, she immediately won the favor of Hegai and everyone who saw her (2:9, 15) For Esther to have won the favor of everyone, she had to have some very special characteristics about herself. It is very hard to please everyone you meet; it seems that no matter how hard you try, there is always someone who does not like something about you.

To win the favor of everyone is not a task that anyone is going to accomplish. However, we should be seeking out to have the favor of God. In 2 Samuel 2:26 Samuel has the favor of God and in Luke 2:52 the young Jesus has the favor of God. It is very important to take a moment to look at how each of these had the favor of God. It seems very understandable that Jesus would have the favor of God, but how about Samuel? He was not the perfect son of God. He was just another boy, right? Samuel's mother Hannah had dedicated and given Samuel back to God after he had opened her womb and allowed her to have a son. In doing so, she gave him back to God. What a sacrifice. His mother did come to see him, but this was not a daily visit. Samuel's time was spent learning, worshiping, and ministering for God, thus winning the favor of God.

We can also win the favor of God, but we are not just going to get it by going through life just relying on being me or you by being you. In Proverbs 2-3 it speaks about gaining favor of God. It starts with wisdom, which we know comes from God. In Proverbs 2:1 it tells us that "if you accept my words and store up my commands within you, turning your ear to wisdom. . .(5) then you will understand the fear of the Lord and find the knowledge of God." To accept God's words we need to be reading them, listening to them and trying to get more and more of them.

During the winter I actually have a little more time to sit around and read a book. When I get into a book, it is really hard to put it down. I want to know more, what is going to happen next? How does the guy end up getting the girl? If reading is not your thing, what about the story that a friend is telling you about what happened last weekend? You hang on to every word, not missing any of the story, wishing you would have been there to see it. This is the same hunger that we are to have for the word of God. The Bible has many examples of how we are to live our lives, how we are to handle tough situations that we are in. Romance stories, using others to get what someone wants, murders, friendships, you name it; it is in there. If your response is: "those stories happened a long time ago; they do not understand what I have to go through now; they did not have the same kinds of trials that I have now." You will be surprised to find it is all in there. Open the Bible up and read it.

The greatest story in the Bible is the main one that we are to accept that God sent His only son Jesus to be born of a virgin, live a perfect life, die a brutal death on the cross and rise again on the third day. Once we have accepted this and believe it with all of our heart and soul, it needs to be written on our hearts. God will give us the hunger to continue to search His word and the understanding. We are to start learning the words and commands that God has laid out for us and start to store them in our hearts.

If you are like me, I have a hard time remembering the "address" of the many scriptures that help me through so many trials; however, the scriptures flow back into the mind at the time I need them the most, and then I can go look them up again. I have index cards that are everywhere my bathroom, bedroom, book bag, work, etc. On these cards are the scriptures that I need the most during this season of my life. There are some seasons that I unfortunately repeat and have to get those index cards full of verses out again, many scriptures can be used for the various seasons I go through. The more that I lean on the word of God, and the more that I seek out His word, the more I am able to apply His truths to my life and situations. As you are seeking the word, ask God for the understanding of His word. He is not the God of confusion. He will give us the wisdom, knowledge and understanding that we need to have (Proverbs 2: 6).

As we gain understanding from God, "We will understand what is right and just and fair-every good path" (Proverbs 2:9). Walking in the good path is not always easy, especially when the world, family, friends, or career have a different one set out for us. As we are walking our paths, God will guide us down the right one. We have to keep seeking out His directions and listening to His voice to be obedient.

Obedience to God's word is a hard one for all of us to follow at times. However, the more that we are in tune with God and actively seeking out His word, the easier it is going to be for us to hear Him versus all of those around us. Proverbs 2 also gives us a warning that if we stray from the paths of God, we will be caught up with those that delight in doing wrong and evil, who are devious, and adulteresses. These will all lead you to death.

We are also to have love and faithfulness. Proverbs 3:3 says that we need to "bind God's words" around your neck, write them on the tablet of your heart." As women we bind a lot of jewelry around our necks. For me my mood, my attire for the day and where I am going influence how big and how much bling I am going to be sporting for that day. We put those objects on to gain attention to them. They are pretty and set off our attire for the day. The love and faithfulness that we have received from God should be shown off the same way. It should be the most "bling" that we have put on for the day. It should be worn in such a way that everyone notices how it shines on us. It is an attention getter and a conversation starter. "Where did you get it? How much did it cost you? Did they have more? Can I borrow it?" We have all heard these questions of our jewelry. What about your most precious one that you can bind around you? Are you hearing these questions about the love and faithfulness from God that you are showing around?

Proverbs 3:4 "Then you will win favor and a good name in the sight of God and man." It is not an easy task, but one that we have to work at. We have to make a daily decision to put the world behind us and seek out God's word and guidance through the day in every situation. We have to try to stay on the straight path when so many are trying to get us to join them, even when it may appear that their path is straight. We must be showing others the love and faithfulness that can only come through us through the love of God. No one ever said that being a Christian was going to be easy. It is a challenge, but the rewards are too numerous to count on list!

# Self Evaluation

Am I constantly seeking to gain the favor of man or that of God?

What has the favor of man gotten me so far? What will it continue to get me?

What rewards will I gain if I have the favor of God?

Have I been seeking out God's word to get knowledge and understanding of my everyday life?

We all have different seasons in our life that we are going through. At this time I am in a season of _____. Find at least 5 scriptures in the Bible that you can rely on to help you get through this season.

Am I in this particular season because I have strayed from the straight path that God desires us to be on? What do I need to purge my life of to get back on the straight path.

Is God's love and faithfulness shining through me? What do I need to do each morning to put in on?

# (Oh, the appearance that I have!)

WE KNOW THAT ESTHER WAS lovely in form and features (2:7), the kind that all the guys stare at and the other girls were jealous of. Every one defines beauty in different ways, physical appearance and the inner being of are two ways to define beauty. In today's society beauty is characterized by your looks, your uniqueness, your body type, and how you dress. Now, you can't say that it was Esther's clothing that screamed look at me, however, when Esther was brought into the palace you can be assured that her clothing has been upgraded from what she had previously worn. According to Encycolopedia.com the people of ancient Persia wore caftans. It was a "loosely-fitted garment with long or short sleeves and could be worn with a belt and the length varied." Women normally wore their hair back and adorned.

Today as young women you are encouraged to "express" yourself, including your dress and adornments. As young Christian women we are to dress with modesty. This does not mean that you do not get to show your personality or your uniqueness in your clothing choices. It does mean that you should be modest, "a mode of dress and deportment intended not to encourage sexual attraction in others" (wikipedia.org). I know that just blew some of your minds; that is the purpose in why you dress in the low cut shirts, short skirts and shorts so short that your gluteus maximus is hanging out. I also know that it is very hard to find clothing at the stores that do not fit this category. So why should you go against the style fashionistas and wear clothing that covers your body? For several good reasons. The very first one is stated in I Corinthians 10:32 "Do not cause anyone to stumble, whether Jews, Greeks or the church of God." Everything we do has a consequence, it can either be beneficial to the glory of God or hinder someone from the glory of God and can even prevent that person from the receiving the salvation of God.

If you are dressed very minimally and show up around the opposite sex, they are not going to be focused on anything except what they can see and what is peeking out at them. Their minds then begin to process what they can do with what you are willing to give and show. Imagine yourself going to church next Sunday. You just purchased a new outfit at the store. It is a very cute skirt (a shear maxi and the solid under layer only goes past your buttocks) and a very cute shear V-neck tank. Sounds cute! Oh! Don't forget your new strappy sandals. Ok, you are a looker, and you pop into church and march up towards the front because you want everyone to see your new outfit, and do they. As you sit down your solid under layer is now not covering your buttocks, and we see your lack of a full pair of panties, and as you bend over to place your purse and Bible on the floor, we can see your toes and everything in between where your V-neck used to be. The men that are witnessing this are now not focusing on the word or God or worshiping, but on the scene you just displayed. Many men do not have control of their thoughts and emotions and are now in a place that they should not be. You may have just caused them to stumble. You may have even caused someone to sin because of having sexual thoughts about you even though they were married, it is considered adultery. Yes, your dress could be the cause of someone committing adultery in his mind.

Now, think of yourself at the feet of Jesus in heaven. He is going through all that you are to be accounted for, and he pauses. He does not say, "well done my good and faithful servant." What is your reaction? Why? The explanation is then, you dressed in a way to tempt others on a daily basis. OUCH! I know that this seems very harsh, but why is it okay to continue to sin over and over with no repentance and expect great and wonderful things from God? Well I can't wear any of the latest trends! WRONG! There are plenty of fashion trends that you can wear and be modest. You just have to put some thought into the style combinations and what will work for your body style. Remember, just because they make it in your size does not mean that it fits your body.

You may have picked up in the scripture that the young ladies that were brought to the palace were to go through 12 months of beauty treatments. Now, that is my type of treatment. Myrrh has been used for years for facial and skin treatments. I like my skin treatments! There is nothing wrong with trying to look beautiful. The problem lies when you are over doing it and it is for the wrong reasons. We all want to be pleasant to the eyes. There are many reasons why women should take the time to "make themselves beautiful." Our skin is exposed to many toxins that have been created in the world and our faces, hands and feet are normally exposed to them all day and almost every day. Those toxins in the air can have very bad effects on us. Our bodies are of the temple that we want the Holy Spirit to reside in (I Corinthians 6:19); therefore, we need to take care of it. Healthy and safe beauty treatments therefore can be very beneficial and relaxing for us.

The young women in the palace also had cosmetics. Yes, makeup. Just like with our clothing, our cosmetics should not be a beacon that screams look at me! Or it should not have people wondering if you just came from your second job as a clown. According to multiple sites from many of the leading make-up companies, they all have a very similar message. Make up should leave you looking polished, "accentuating" the positives and hiding the flaws." It takes practice to get down the colors and techniques for your own facial coloring and shape. So, have fun with it, get some girlfriends together and have a party. Go on a trip to the mall and let the experts show you. There is nothing wrong with enjoying learning how to wear the makeup properly. Don't be wearing it to draw attention to yourself, but for people to look at you and say "WOW! She has it all together."

# Self Evaluation

What clothes are in my closet that I wear? What are they revealing?

Can I put together different ensembles than I normally wear so that they are covering more of my body.

Do I need to ask God to forgive me for the way that I have been dressing because I could be causing others to stumble/sin?

Am I encouraging my friends to dress in ways that are too revealing?

Do I know how to properly apply my cosmetics? Am I the latest clown?

# But I Did All the Work!

WHILE IN SCHOOL, IT SEEMS like the teachers love to assign group projects, getting us to start to work well as a member of a team. The problem is you always have the same type of people in the groups: the one who takes the project over, the one that does nothing, the one that says that they will do much more than they actually do, and the one that talks nonstop through the entire process. I don't know which category you fall into, but you also know that the majority of the time it seems like a miracle that you receive a decent grade on your project. Then you learn that another actually receives the credit for the work that you put into the project. This burns you to the core. No recognition for your part of the project whether it was hard work or not is very aggravating.

Esther very easily could have taken the credit for saving the king; instead, she gave the credit were the credit was due (Esther 2:22). Mordecai was not in the palace as Esther was telling the king about the plot that had been discovered about his assassination, so Mordecai would have never known that the credit was not given to him. So many times we want to look good to others and please them. We tend to become very jealous at times of the recognition that others receive.

In teaching the children's classes at church, many times there are siblings in the classes together. It just so happens that the Wednesday night class has three siblings together ranging from ages 6 to 14. They are all three boys, very active but good boys. It never fails though; the two oldest are always doing something to get the littlest one in trouble. For some reason when he is getting caught his brothers have already fled the scene. It is like they know the exact moment that he is going to be caught. He always looks so pitiful when he is caught; he never tells me that it was anyone else's fault or tries to get out of the situation. He stands there and takes whatever I say to him and then he goes on about his way.

This little boy could have easily put the blame where it was due, but he took credit for something that was not completely his to take credit for. These are two completely different situations, but both very important. To take the credit for what someone else has done to receive the glory and benefits is very selfish of a person. Galatians 5:20 lets us know that selfish ambition is an act of sinful nature. We are to be living by the Spirit and our fruits should be those fruits of the Spirit. Once we accept Jesus Christ as our Lord and Savior we should no longer take joy in the sinful nature that we are born into. Now are there going to be times that we slip up and make mistakes, yes, but we need to be constantly aware that we are making mistakes and trying to correct them. We should also have a feeling that we are doing something wrong if we are in a situation that we are taking credit for something that is not our to take.

Then, there are times that we accept the responsibility for the situation to protect others, or we are taking the responsibility for the entire situation and not sharing it with others. The little boy in the class could easily have ratted out his two brothers, however, he did not and took the "tongue lashings" and went on to play with them again. It takes a lot of self-control and goodness to take responsibility for your actions. It takes you a step farther to take it for yourself and others that are involved. I do not know how many of us would actually stand up and take the responsibility for others. While I was growing up, if I got caught doing anything, I blamed my little brother whether he was involved or not. I did not have any problems or second thoughts about allowing him to be the one who would get into trouble. Praise God that this is not the mentality that Jesus had! Can you imagine the outcome if he did? If He would have gotten to the cross and cried out to God, "Father, Let them each be responsible for their own sins! I was free of sin and will not take the punishment for them!" We would not be free of our sins, and I certainly do not want all the punishment that I deserve for all the sins that I have committed.

So an unselfish behavior is one that we should seek. It is not going to be an easy task. Many of us are going to have to work at it. It is often as hard to give people the praise that they desire to hear for doing something good. We all like to be recognized for things we have done, but are we recognizing those who are doing things for us? I know that cards and letters are a thing of the past, but it used to be when someone did something for you or you received a gift, you sent a thank you card to that person. It was an inexpensive way to let them know that you appreciated their time and money that they spent on you. Now, with technology, emails and texts are the normal modes of communication; however, are we using them for recognition or just ramblings? I can get so caught up with making sure that people are meeting the expectations that I can easily forget that there are several that are going above and beyond everyday that need recognized for their works. A little recognition will go a long way.

# Self Evaluation

Galatians 5:17-22 describes the fruits of sinful nature, look at each one and determine whether or not you are allowing them to have control over parts of your life:

> Sexual Immorality
> Impurity and debauchery
> Idolatry and witchcraft
> Hatred
> Discord
> Jealousy
> Fits of Rage
> Selfish Ambition
> Dissensions
> Factions
> Envy
> Drunkenness
> Orgies

Are you allowing the fruits of Spirit to lead your desires and passions?

Are you routinely stepping in and taking the credit that others deserve?

This week what opportunities have you had to recognize people around you? Did you take advantage of that opportunity and recognize them? If not, stop and do it now. Send them a text or a note thanking them for what they did.

# I Can Do It Myself

I HAVE A VERY HARD time taking advice from someone else. If I have sought out the advice of others I am very accepting of it and try to do what they suggested. However, as soon as people start to tell me what I need to do with my life, behavior, dress, you name it, I become very defensive. I think that you have decided that you are out to get me and you don't like me. It is very easy to take a simple suggestion and blow it up into a situation that I can turn around in my mind and convince myself that there was nothing simple about it at all. While in high school I thought that I needed to be involved in every activity. I was the president or vice-president of multiple school clubs and a co-captain of the soccer team. Additionally I was involved in activities outside of school. My parents, teachers and friends tried to warn me several times that I was putting too much on my plate. The all were giving me suggestions of how to be involved in all the different clubs and which ones to make my priority. I was convinced that I could be in charge of all of them and do great things in all of them without any problems at all. What I did not understand was that all the advice that I was receiving would have saved me a lot of time, embarrassment, and integrity if I had listened. Instead I locked down and rammed my way through.

My parents had to talk the school into not "flunking" me because I was missing too many days of school for activities. I was not getting my homework done until time for class to start the next day. The clubs were not accomplishing great things, and the teacher sponsors were doing the majority of the work that needed to be done. I had made a mess of everything. I truly feel sorry for the mess that I left the next year to pick up. They had a lot of work to catch up on because nothing was done whole-heartedly by me. I allowed myself to be pulled in too many directions.

To this day I still have a hard time taking the advice from others when I am not seeking it out. It may be a control issue; it could be an independence issue, or name it what you would like. I know that I have a problem, I have to pray daily for God to help me with these specific issues prior to me entering the workforce. Many of the people that are offering advice to us are not doing it maliciously. They are our friends and family who from the outside looking in tend to see something that we are missing from our tunnel vision. There are also times that I receive "guidance" from others that I can not respond to. I have learned that if I am receiving unasked for advice to not respond immediately. I may go and cry about it. I may get angry about it and blame others. But in the long run if I clear my head of my thoughts, and get rid of the delivery of it, many times there are good ideas laced in the middle of what was said. It takes a lot of prayer and time to clear my head, but I can sometimes get there.

Esther was willing to receive the advice from others and follow what they suggested. In 2:10 it states that "Esther had not revealed her nationality and family background, because Mordecai had forbidden her to do so." I am sure that was not always an easy task to do. Girls talk! As soon as we are closed up in a room together for any length of time we start to talk, small talk to start with. The more time we spend together, the more information we share with others about ourselves. Esther's background would have been very important to her; however, if she would have shared that information, we do not know exactly what would have happened to her, but it could not have been good. Esther, even though what she was told to do was hard, followed the instructions.

Esther was under the care of Hegai in the harem. She had been under his care for 12 months (it took 12 months of beauty treatments before a girl could go before the king). In the 12 month time frame, they would have gotten to know each other and from what we can gather, they developed a trusting relationship with one another. In 2:15 it tells us that Esther "asked for nothing other than what Hegai, suggested."

Esther had the option to choose anything she wanted to wear on her night to meet the king. I can picture it now, a room as big as my house, the finest silk clothing lining all the walls, shoes/sandals to match each one, the finest gold and gemstone jewelry in every color imaginable, and adornments for the hair in all textures, stones, and gems. WHAT A CLOSET! One that a girl could become lost in for days. One in which you could easily overdo the outfit. However, Esther only asked for what was suggested to her. Hegai would have known what the king liked in his women how he liked them dressed, how he liked their hair fixed. These were the suggestions that Esther heard from Hegai, listened to and then followed.

It takes a lot of self discipline to be able to accept willing and openly the advice from others. Proverbs 12:1 states, "Whoever loves discipline loves knowledge, but he who hates correction is stupid." The advice that we receive from others will help us grow in knowledge. That knowledge may be about a job, skill, or even ourselves. But if we never accept the correction that others have to offer us, we will never grow. Correction is going to come from everyone and everywhere, even from the Holy Spirit.

None of us want to be lacking in anything, especially in wisdom. The world is becoming a very technical world, and many feel that if do not keep up with the latest in electronics, they are lacking. This could be the farthest thing from the truth. You see we need to be able to grow in our wisdom. Proverbs 19:20 says, "Listen to advice and accept instruction, and in the end you will be wise." We can learn a great deal from those that are wiser than us people that have actually tried what we are trying; people who are there to train us for a job because they are the best around at what they do. We are going to learn more from people that are excelling because they have gone through trial and error to learn how to properly handle situations. We all get tired of hearing our parents tell us, "this is how it happened when I was your age." The people, language and setting may have changed since then, but the outcome will be very similar when it comes to thoughts, feelings, skills or knowledge.

At work I find it very interesting to watch the new workers come in. Some are very quiet and have no confidence in their skills, some are willing to ask a million questions, and others do not ask any questions or want any help because they already know the basics and they can do it on their own. We tend to judge the quiet ones: are they really ready? Do they know anything? Are they book smart but lacking the skills? Those that know it all: they are going to get a reality check when a crisis happens, I am not helping them when they get into trouble because they did not want my help to begin with. We label these workers and don't always care if they make it or not. However, that are willing to ask questions and seek help from those that have been doing the job, those are more willing to help and guide. These are the ones that we are wanting to see succeed. Is it right? Absolutely not! We should be willing to help and guide all, no matter what their personality or confidence level is.

As people we gravitate more to those that want our help and are willing to listen to us. Esther was willing to listen to Hagai; it states in 2:9 that she "won his favor." It does not say how that actually happened, but I like to think that Esther was not a quiet girl, nor was she a know it all that was telling everyone else in the harem what to do. She was probably scared but willing to listen to the guidance of the one who was over them.

Listening to others is a hard trait for many of us to demonstrate. Many of us speak before we listen which in turn gets us into misunderstandings. If we cannot listen to those around us, how are we going to listen to God when He speaks to us? God is not screaming back at us and beating us over the head to get our attention. He is there guiding us down the right path to take. But for us to go down this right path, we have to be listening to His voice. When we decide to not listen to it and do things on our own, we are going to stray off of God's path and onto our own. I read a sentence in a book once that was very powerful to me and has stuck with me. It stated, "If you can not obey the authorities around you, how are you ever going to obey the authority of God?" To obey these authorities, you must listen to them. Listening is going to take practice, especially if you are not used to doing it. It is something that each person has to make a conscious effort to do.

Now that I know that I am needing to accept the advice of others and listen, I try to make a conscious effort to do so. I do not always succeed in accomplishing it, but when a mess up, I am aware that I actually messed up this time. I can then figure out what I did wrong and try to correct it. Just like our relationship with God, once we are actively working on listening and trying to follow His guidance, if we mess up, we are more likely to understand and hear from Him that we need to get back on His path. God is forgiving when we mess up. Thank goodness, because I do it a lot. But unlike those around us who may get tired of giving the same advice over and over, God will keep reminding us!

# Self Evaluation

When I receive advice from others when I am not asking for it, what is my typical response?

How is this response different from the response that I have when I receive advice from others when I ask for it?

Am I willing to evaluate the advice that they give at a later time to see what parts of it I am willing to accept?

How can I change my normal response to "unwanted" advice to be able to pray about it and discover what God would have me change or accept?

When I try to make a change based on the advice that someone gives me, do I stick to it, even when it is hard?

What type of personality do I have towards others around me? Am I quiet and withdrawn, do I ask questions and seek guidance of others, or do I know it all and refuse to ask questions? You may have some of all of these. Can you determine in what situations you are more likely to follow each path? If you can identify those situations, pray that God will help you be aware of these situations and help you slow down to listen.

# You Need to Look For
# Someone Else Lord

ESTHER DID NOT ALWAYS JUMP at the first suggestion
that she received to do what others asked of her. She
sometimes had an excuse not to do what was asked of her. We
do not have the words that Esther sent back to Mordecai, but
we have his response to her reply. In Esther 4: 13-14 "he sent
back this answer: "Do you not think that because you are in
the king's house you alone of all the Jews will escape. For if
you remain silent at this time, relief and deliverance for the
Jews will arise from another place, but you and your father's
family will perish. And who knows but that you have come
to royal position for such a time as this." She had Mordecai,
all stirred up.

So many times we do not like the challenge that is
requested of us whether from others or from God. We have
many excuses to not step up and follow the will of God in
our lives. As a young adult I accepted the call into ministry at
church camp. I did not know what direction exactly God was
calling me, but I knew it was into the ministery. As I finished
high school and then moved away to college, I kept moving
farther and farther from God. I knew in my heart that I was

called to be in the ministry, but I was not doing anything to meet the challenge that God had placed in my life. I would visit the Baptist Student Ministry when they had a special event and when they were giving away free food. I would visit local churches but did not feel "comfortable" at them and even ended up attending a few different denominations. I was struggling; spiritually I was in a full battle within myself a battle that I had started.

You see, when we know that we are supposed to be doing the will of God, and we know that He has chosen us to do His work, and we run. . . . eventually we get tired of running. Our legs start to cramp, our lungs are burning, and our minds are spiraling, trying to get us to stop. We can stop running or we can keep pushing ourselves until our body finally stops from exhaustion. Sound familiar?

You are not the only one that God gives a challenge to. He is going to challenge all of His children. If it was easy to complete the task of God's work, who would get all the credit? We would. Instead, God gives us challenges that are beyond our normal ability. This is a great opportunity for us to give Him all of the credit for the work that is being done. We are just the vessels that He is using for His glory.

Let's take a look at Moses. You were probably prepared to skip the next few paragraphs thinking that it was going to be about Jonah. He is another great example of what happens when you run from God. There is nothing like getting swallowed by a giant fish and living in it's belly for a few days. I cannot even imagine the smell that one would have to overcome. But, back to Moses. When Moses had fled Egypt and was tending the sheep in Horeb, he came across the burning bush. I do thoroughly enjoy Exodus 3-4 because it describes all the excuses that Moses has not to do God's will. Sounding familiar?

Exodus 3:11 says "But Moses said to God, "Who am I, that I should go to Pharaoh and bring the Israelites out of Egypt?" This is Moses first excuse to God. We all use this excuse. Who am I, God, to go? I do not have enough money, unlike someone else. I do not have enough vacation time built up at work. I have bills that I need to pay. I am not well liked and no one is going to listen to me. I don't know anyone that lives where you are calling me to go. Who am I? We all can easily compare ourselves to someone else we know or have heard of those that already are doing great and mighty things for God. Those that are making friends and money everywhere they go. I am a no-body! This is one of the greatest lies that the Devil can get everyone of us to believe. If he is successful in getting us to believe that we are a nobody and there is someone better to do what God has called us to do, the Devil has won that battle and has prevented someone from hearing the message of God.

God did not let Moses just throw that excuse out and accept it. God tells Moses in verse 12, "I will be with you." And this will be the sign to you that it is I who have sent you: When you have brought the people out of Egypt, you will worship God on this mountain." This is a promise of God to be a sustainer and a protector of Moses, that He is the "I Am." God is also letting Moses know what one of the end results would be. There is only one I AM and that I AM, the one and only, is telling Moses that He is the one that will be with Moses.

Many times when we are called to do something, we are braver and more willing to complete it if someone is willing to come with us and stand beside us. Even on nights that I am home, if my husband is home with me I don't have a care in the world, but as soon as I am on my own, my senses go crazy and I am a nervous wreck. Even if the kids are home with me, I am braver because I am not alone in this big house. Likewise everyday, if we are going through the day without God, we are at risk, at risk for the enemy to grab hold of us and at risk for us to be scared while we are trying to get through the day. But if we realize that we are not alone and God is with us, we can stand tall and feel the bravery of having God with us and guiding us through.

Knowing that God was going to be with him, Moses still had excuses. Verse 13 says "Suppose I go to the Israelites and say to them, 'The God of your fathers has sent me to you,' and they ask me, 'What is his name?' Then what shall I tell them?" Moses knows if he goes to the Israelites that they are going to listen to him. The last time that he was seen in Egypt, he killed an Egyptian. His odds for a safe return were probably not in his favor. One could also speculate that the Israelites would have a hard time believing that God had sent him. They are in slavery at this time. I would think that as slaves, they are having a hard time having a relationship with God. Even when things are going well for the Israelites, they run away from God.

God tells Moses He is "I AM WHO I AM." This is what you are to say to the Israelites: 'I AM has sent me to you,'" vs. 14. God has already told Moses that He is going to be with him, but his is now telling him that it is HE that is sending him. God is the one that is dependable, faithful and the one that you can trust. He is the truth and the Lord. Moses is being sent to the Israelites by the greatest authority that could send him. God also tells Moses of things that He will do to the Egyptians if the Israelites are not freed. The things that Moses now has the knowledge of could only come from God. These are not things that just anyone would have the knowledge of. These are truths of the future that could only come from God.

As God is calling us to go and to do we need to remember that He is still the "I AM." God is still has the greatest authority in heaven or earth, and only HE knows the truth of our future. God calls all of us to spread the gospel the truths of the gospel are very powerful and gives us a peace and wisdom that can only come from God. Many of us do not know exactly what God has planned for our future or where we are going to be. We are to remember that only God knows our future; it is our responsibility to keep our hearts and ears open to the I AM. It is not easy to wait for God's answer as to who we are to be and what we are to be doing. My husband and I are in that season of our lives now. We know that we are to be in the ministry; my husband is called to preach, and I love women's ministry. However, God is working us over right now. I do not know where we are going to end up, but God is definitely doing some major pruning in our lives as individuals and as a family. It is very easy right now to have excuses, but we must keep building our relationship with our Lord.

It is not enough that God has told Moses that He will be with him and that He is the I AM. Moses' next excuse is: "What if they do not believe me or listen to me and say, 'The Lord did not appear to you'?" 4:I. This sounds like something my children would say as an excuse. "But they are not going to believe me!" No one is going to believe that I did that great paper, that I was able to get those resources for someone in need. That I was able to . . . you can fill in the blank. You may have already used this excuse.

God answered by using common items to perform uncommon events. God used Moses' staff by turning it into a snake, turned Moses' hand leprous, and turned water into blood. You and I and our possessions on earth are very common; however, God uses each and every one of us to perform uncommon events in His name if we are willing. We are used to plant the seeds of His gospel. There are so many that are in need not only of physical things but have spiritual needs as well. We, many times, are willing to fill those physical needs, but do not or are not willing to help the person with her spiritual needs. We use many excuses about not having the talents needed or not being spiritual enough ourselves to help others. But, dear sister, all God is asking for is the vessel, you. He will then do the miraculous things through you and the things that you have. You just have to be willing to use yourself and what you have. God is telling us that He is the one that can perform miracles. . .why are we getting in the way? Yes Lord, I am willing for you to use me. Please let me see your miracles performed through me! Is there a greater gift that we could give someone?

For every excuse that Moses has, God has a better answer for him, but he is still not getting it. God wants Moses to do a specific job for him. He does not want someone else

He wants Moses! If we asked someone to perform a task for us and they come up with multiple excuses, we are going to stop asking them and perform it ourselves. We are not going to have patience with them. This time Moses uses "O Lord, I have never been eloquent, neither in the past nor since you have spoken to you servant. I am slow of speech and tongue." vs.10. This one I have heard a thousand times from lots of different people. "I don't like to talk in front of people. I get tongue tied when I am talking. I am not as smart as them." I could keep going. You have probably used many of these!

My poor husband, when he first accepted God's call to become a preacher, he also did not like to speak in front of people. He hated the speech classes that he took in college and was very nervous. When he first started, he would hold a pen in his hand while he was teaching. It only took one session of that for me to take all writing instruments away from him. The entire time that he was speaking, he was tapping the pen on the side of the podium, driving me crazy. Once we removed the pen, there were lots of um's being used in every sentence. This also about did me in. But the poor guy, he has kept going, growing in his speech in front of others. Now he does not hold items, does not have near the um's, and does not even use notes as he allows the word of God to flow through his vessel. It was a great challenge for him and a fear that he had to overcome, just like you can.

I am not just going to pick on my husband; I have issues in front of others also. They are just a different group of issues. I was raised basically being in front of others. Growing up my brother and I were taken everywhere our parents went, and they were involved in everything. Not only were they involved, but for many of the organizations where they worked or volunteered, they were in charge. This put my brother and me in a very public position to learn many skills. Speaking in front of a group of people has not really bothered me except that I get nervous about the message and do not want to confuse anyone. In the past when I was starting to speak to more groups became I cocky. I was over confident in the message that I was going to deliver whether it was at school, work, or church. It got to be I did not even take notes or have an outline. I would just "wing it." This did not work out well, and my presentations were a mess and not at all effective. God had to "get a hold of me" and get my senses shaken back into me. That is definitely humbling!

If you are one that is not confident to speak in from of others, or like me and at times overly confident, we need to remember that God is going to teach us what to say. Exodus 3:11 says 'The Lord said to him, "Who gave man his mouth? Who make him deaf or mute? What gives him sight or makes him blind? Is it not I, the Lord? Now go; I will help you speak and will teach you what to say." God is reminding Moses that He is the one that created everything about him. God can take away his voice, hearing or sight at anytime. God is the one that gave us our mouth, ears and eyes, and He is the one that decided who is going to use each one in specific ways. If we do not want to use the gifts that God has given us, He can take them away.

"O Lord, please send someone else to do it." This is Moses' plea in Exodus 3:13. Now we all know that God has a great deal of patience and is slow to anger; however, God has had it at this point. Verse 13 tells us that "the Lord's anger burned against Moses." Now we know that we have read about many incidents in the Bible where the Lord was angry, many times even at groups of people. God has been talking one on one with Moses who keeps giving him excuse after excuse to not do something and God has just had it!

I can get to this point with my children or even at work when we are trying to accomplish a new task and we are months into it and they still keep going back into their old ways. I can not imagine what it would have been like to have God so angry at Moses. Did he raise his voice like parents do? Did he shake his head at him? Did he point his finger at him? God finally tells Moses that Aaron who speaks well is going to go with him. He will now not be physically alone as he goes to Egypt. What frustration God must have had with Moses. Notice that in all the prior responses from God, He has pointed out who He is, His authority, His constant presence, His miracles, His truth and knowledge and His creation. This time he offers another to be with him.

What is God calling you to do, or where is He asking you to go? Have you gone through all the excuses that Moses has? I truly believe that God is still showing his patience for me. He has told me many times to complete a specific task for him, and I have allowed the world to influence my time so I am prevented from doing it. I allow my wants and needs to be placed before God's directions. If we continue to refuse to do what God is asking us to do, He is going to give it to someone that is willing. What blessings are you willing to lose out on because you are full of excuses? As the story continues, Moses is not the one that speaks to the elders of the Israelites; it is Aaron, and they heard him. You would think that this could bring mixed emotions for Moses as he watches and hears Aaron speak and then the elders listen to him. For us it could also bring many mixed emotions including jealousy of the other that God has sent to help us.

Esther did not have as many excuses as Moses when she was asked to go forth. Her next step should be one that all of us grasp and follow. She asked for fasting and a gathering of all the Jews in Susa. She did not ask them for a specific outcome or guidance. She asked to be lifted up! When God is calling us, instead of having excuse after excuse, we need to have focused prayer and ask others to be lifting us up in prayer. We do not have tell them all the details. Many times we do not know the details ourselves yet, but others can be lifting us up. There is still power in prayer. I see the power of prayer on a daily basis in the hospital and in many churches. Allow others to lift you up.

I witnessed a great and mighty movement of God recently in a church that I love to visit. During the invitation people were going to the altar and sharing with the church the struggles they have faced in their lives that very week. Some had been ongoing and some were new realizations of struggles, but they came in front of many people, broken and wounded. Those in the church did not shake and lower their heads; they did not belittle them for not being perfect; they did not discourage them for doing what God was calling them to do. The church filled the altar and surrounded these individuals and raised them up in prayer. What a wonderful work God is doing in that church and with the members there! This may be too much for you or to dramatic if so find a few people that God has put in your life that you know will lift you up, and let them assist you in sharing God's work.

Dear sister, stop making excuses! Allow God to show you that He is the I AM, that He never will leave you, and He will do great and mighty things through you. Allow God to use the talents you have, the ones He gave you to be the one that plants the seeds in many. I can't plant seeds you say. Then maybe you are tilling the soil, maybe you are watering the seeds, maybe you are pulling weeds! Just like God gave Moses and Esther the courage needed to go before the earthly authorities, He will give you the courage you need to go forth!

# Self Evaluation

Are you currently giving God excuses? You may not even realize anymore that you have excuses because you have used them so many times. Spend time in prayer asking God to show the excuses and barriers that you are using to prevent His work from being done through you.

Are you taking the time to listen to God's answers to your excuses? We have to stop what we are doing to listen to God's answers. Has God been proving to you who He is and why He wants you?

What wonderful things has God been doing for you that you have not responded to or given him the credit for?

Do you need to work on having courage? God will give you the courage that you need to step forward with to complete what He is calling you to do.

Identify a handful of people that you know and trust who will truly prayer for you when you ask them. List them here.

Let these people know that you have identified them to be a go to when you are in need of prayer. For clarification from God or courage to do what He is calling you to do.

Have you been jealous of others in your life that have stepped in and completed what God was calling you to do? Spend time in prayer asking God to show you these people that you need to ask forgive from God. Don't be mad or jealous of them for doing what God was originally calling you to do.

Find scriptures to write down and keep with you during seasons that God is calling on you. You might find some for courage, some about excuses, and some about listening to God. Remember that scripture is the living word of God. Listen to what He is trying to tell you.

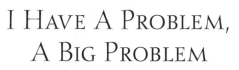

# I Have A Problem,
# A Big Problem

ESTHER HAD A PROBLEM, A big problem. She was
faced with a problem that could wipe out an entire
nation. Many times we think that we are in a tough situation,
and many times we are. We allow ourselves to make our
own decisions, which then do nothing but get us into a big
mess. We are faced each and everyday with challenges that
are spiritual, physical, emotional and/or financial. Often we
think that we are the only ones around that have ever dealt
with this type of problem.

I am very good at getting myself into messes. I think
that I am able to make decisions that are the best with the
information that is presented to me about a problem. That is
what I tell others anyway. "I can only make the best decision
with the information that is present at the time." Truth be
told, this is the worst type of decision that I can make. Many
times as I have the information presented to me, I make an
immediate decision and take the actions that I believe should
happen.

If Esther would have made an immediate decision and
gone straight to the king, the outcome could be completely

different. As Esther stated in 4:11 anyone that approaches the king in his court without being summoned was looking at death. Instead, Esther tried to not have to deal with the problem the first go round. Mordecai was able to emphasize to Esther that she did need to deal with the problem.

At work I many times have to deal with people that are at their worst. They are struggling with anger, grief, frustration, any negative feeling you can image. These people will often take their emotions out on those that are caring for them. Even though we all understand that they are in a very difficult time in their lives, people still wanted to be treated kindly. Many times I do not step in immediately hoping that the situation will work its self out. Maybe it was that moment they received bad news, maybe personalities had to be adjusted to cope with one another, whatever it was I always hope that people are "big" enough to take of the situation on their own.

Unfortunately, many times people are not able to "handle" their own emotions and they become out of control and lash out continuously at those around them. I, then, must step in often. I cannot "fix" what has caused them have their emotions, but we have to come to an agreement of how to be together for the next short time in their life. These situation are difficult to address, and finding the right words and tone can be tricky. It takes time and careful thought to be able to complete successfully. When I first started handling these situations, I was very young and had the mentality that if you did not see it my way then I could have you removed and we no longer had to put up with you. I felt that one way or another it was a winning situation for me and my staff.

In the long run, this did not fix anything, and it probably caused issues that I never saw.

Esther's problem was not going to go away either. I know that her problem was much bigger than the ones in my example; however, her approach is one that I and many others have had to learn to follow the hard way. Just like in my example, I like to think that if I stand back the problem will correct itself. Our problems are not going to correct themselves! If anything, when we ignore them they tend to get worse.

I was visiting a church with my family recently and oh how the Holy Spirit was moving. During the 45 minute invitation a young women came up and confessed that she had a sin of silence, not one that many of us think about. But this young women got me to thinking. She stated that while at a wrestling tournament with her son there was a Buddha statue. Many had commented on the fact that there was a Buddha statue there and no other religious symbols or statues were present. Many conversations at the wrestling meet and on the way home were made, but she never once brought up Jesus Christ during any of the conversations.

You see, many times we know how we feel. We know if something is right or wrong. We know that one voice can make a difference, but we say nothing! Esther could have easily said nothing and sat back and allowed silence to try to fix the problem fortunately, she didn't do that. We have already spoken of wisdom, wisdom that we are to ask God for. Through the wisdom that God will give us, his power will be demonstrated. This wisdom will not come from man, but from God. Paul claimed, it was not of himself or the wisdom that he had gained from man, but the wisdom and power of the Holy Spirit and God in his life 1 Corinthians 2:4-5. That allowed him to stay focused on the God.

The sin of silence can also destroy you. In Psalm 32 King David is writing specifically of the sin of silence. He stated in 32:3 "When I kept silent, my bones wasted away through my groaning all day long." If we know that we are to say something and not be silent, we will have conviction in our lives regarding what we should have done. Many times as we watch the situation unfold or worsen the grief that we are carrying around will only get worse because we did not say what we were "called" to say.

Esther did not remain silent; however, she did not speak immediately. She instead fasted and had all those around her and the Jews fast also. She prepared and prayed for the correct action to take and the right thing to say. When she did make the first move, she did not go in presenting herself as a slob or unprepared. She put on her "royal robes and stood in the inner court" Esther 5:1. She came prepared and willing to present herself as a royal; her presence was noticed by the king and he accepted her.

Many times we just want to blurt out the problem and the "appropriate" way to fix the problem. In 5:3 Esther had the opportunity to bring the problem to the king and lay it all at his feet, however, she bought more time and knew how to get the king's attention by getting his curiosity going. If we were to go running into a situation and just blurting out information many times we are going to get the information jumbled up and make the situation more confusing than it needs to be. Plus we are going to make ourselves look unwise in the situation.

To be prepared to address a problem does not mean to arm ourselves with information that is going to hurt those around us or throw items back in their faces. Esther presented the problem to the king as one that he saw as wrong. Having seen that an entire population of people would be annihilated was easy to see when presented with the facts. He immediately wanted to fix the problem and know who was responsible for it. Esther brought forth a plea for herself and the lives of all her fellow Jews. She even admitted that she would not have troubled the king if they were to go back into slavery (7:4), but this was for their lives, murder.

Esther's choices were not common. She was not given options where she could follow someone else's advice or guidance on. The choice to not do anything would lead to many people dying. I am sure that decision would be a very hard one to live with day in and day out, that is saying, if she was the one Jew to actually survive. The other option put her life on the line immediately by going before the king uninvited. When I am making decisions, options that might leave me with any type of injury are normally removed immediately! I do not like pain or conflict, so those options are out. Many of the decisions we have to make are not ones that those around us may of come up with or would say are "safe." We need to be seeking out the choice that God has for us to get through a situation.

Many times the choice that God has for us will have us stepping out on a limb. It may be more like a twig that is bending under us, but it is the twig that God gave us to hold on to. God is going to lead the way for us and guide us through the situations, but we must be willing to follow. He tells us in Exodus 23:2 "do not follow the crowd in doing wrong," 1 Peter 2:21 says "Christ suffered for you, leaving you an example, that you should follow in his steps." It is easy to follow the crowd, but they are not the ones that died for you nor can they lead you into doing what is right and good. Only the one that suffered and died for YOU and ME can lead us and guide us.

Esther could have easily picked up and left. She could have ignored the problem all together and not ever have addressed it. Being the queen, I am sure that she had access to get out of the borders of the king's control. She could have fled, but the problem would have overcome her. The mind games that we allow to play out would have probably led to her death, knowing that she possibly could have done something other than run and see her people all killed.

Joshua 24:14-15 "Now fear the Lord and serve him with all faithfulness. Throw away the gods your forefathers worshiped beyond the river and in Egypt, and serve the Lord. But if serving the Lord seems undesirable to you, then choose for yourselves this day whom you will serve, whether the gods your forefathers served beyond the River, or the gods of the Amorites, in whose land you are living. But as for me and my household, we will serve the Lord." We have a choice to make. Do you want to run from your problems and allow others to be making decisions for you? Do you want to allow the world and fear to be making your decisions for you? Or are you allowing God to show you the choices that you are to make.

God made it very clear to the Israelites, and He is making it very clear to us. Are we serving Him or the world? If we are serving God, then we are going to seek out His guidance for us when we have a trial/problem. God wants to be in control. God allows us to have trials in our lives, trials that are bigger than what you and I can fix or control. There is a reason for this! There are only two ways to get out of these: 1. Do it ourselves and create bigger messes or 2. Allow God to pull us through as only He can do. Philippians 4:13 is a verse that we all know, "I can do everything through Him who gives me strength." The verse does not say that it is through my strength, but only that of God!

I would not be able to hold on to that little twig that I mentioned earlier at all on my own. On my own I am weak (Ok, very weak); it is only through God's strength that I am able to hold on to it! Esther also could not do anything on her own. She had to ask for all the Jews to fast with her. She knew that it was very important for her to rely on God and those that were also believers to lift her up. We also need to be surrounding ourselves with those that are believers and have a relationship with God so they can lift us up. How many times have you been asked by someone to pray for them and you said Ok, but you never said a prayer for them? How much confidence are you going to have and how much prayer is going out for you if you ask people to pray for you that don't have a relationship with God and are never lifting you up?

Esther ends up being victorious and saves many lives just by speaking up. You and I may not be saving many lives, but we are still called to speak up and not just allow problems to grow. However, we are not to get involved in every other person's problems and try to get them out of them. We can pray for them and be a source that someone can confide in. If someone comes to us for assistance, we need to point them to the one and only one they can truly place all their trust in for their problems and that is God. To trust in someone you must know that person. You are not going to trust someone that you do not know. Do you know God? Do you have a relationship with Him is, you can put that trust in Him?

Esther had to face the rationale of what could happen to her. All the rationale that she could muster would have told her, "No, don't do it." Many of our decisions in life are not based on rational choices. Is it rational that God would leave heaven, a perfect and beautiful city to come to earth, that He would live and walk amongst the sinners, that He would die for you and me to save us from our own sins? The answers that God has for us may not seem rational to us, but He has a plan for everything. Many times we do not understand it or know why the challenges is being given to us, but remember it is for the glory of God. Are you ready to face the challenge!

# Self Evaluation

What is your first response to a problem? Do you try to get out of dealing with the problem all together?

What it the normal outcome of trying to get out of the problem?

Am I committing a sin of silence? You may have committed the sin of silence so much that you no longer see it as a problem. The sin of silence is still sin, there are times that we must speak up and address the problem. Do you know of others that have told you about a sin of silence and were convicted by the Holy Spirit because of it?

When I have a problem, do I just blurt out responses and ways to fix the problem to others? Am I giving the best possible solutions or advise in my hasty responses?

Am I a prayer? We should always keep an open line of communication with God, but many times when we have issues we keep them to ourselves. Why I am not sharing them with God? He already knows everything that we do, say, etc, so why are we not telling Him about our problems and where we need assistance?

Do I have an open line with God? If not, let's start now. Take this time to speak to God and let Him know of a problem that you having right now. He does not care the size of the problem. You just need to give it to Him.

I need to prepare myself to handle problems that I am facing. I am needing to dig into God's word for Him to guide through what I need to do. Take this time to find scriptures that will help guide you through your current situation. Write these verses down and keep them with you.

DEAR SISTER, I KNOW THAT all this could have seemed overwhelming, you may have it already figured out, or you may not think that you will ever be in these situations that I have given you throughout this study. If someone would have explained it all to me early in my life, I would have acknowledged it all, agreed with them and then moved on with my life and still made my own decisions. Truth be told, there is a little of Esther in all of us. As young women we all have a secret desire to be loved and treasured as a queen by someone. We all want to be pampered. None of us wants to be in a constant state of turmoil, allowing situations or problems define us. The mistakes that I have made, you may not have ever been faced with. I pray that we are never faced with the problem that Esther had where the fate of others is in our hands.

I do know that the Lord God is the one that will teach us true love, He is the one that we can trust, He is the one with whom we need to establish a relationship. Philippians 4:13 says, "I can do everything through him who gives me strength." It is the strength of God that will get us through, not that of our own. As a young woman I have made several mistakes and continue to make mistakes. It is my prayer for myself and for all young women that we learn to lean on God and not man to get us through every day.

You may have picked up on many more tidbits that you could learn from Esther. My prayer is that you have written them down and will continue to study them. Remember that the Bible is the living word of God. God may be revealing other things to you. Each time I pick up the Bible and read it, more is revealed to me. We all claim at different times in our lives that we are the only ones that have ever gone through situations. Just remember that you can pick up the Bible and find it in there. No matter how far we have come, we also have farther to go and more to learn. God has a purpose for each and everyone of us. Some have found it already and some of us are stilling trying to find what we are supposed to be doing for the kingdom of God.

You may have done this study because your friend wanted you to do it with her and you have never had a relationship with God. You may being saying that this is something that you do not want. I can assure you that there is a void in your life. You may be filling that void with shopping, people, boys, drugs, alcohol, sex, etc. The only thing is the void is never gone. We are created with a desire for more. The more is only going to be filled with GOD.

There are many ways to learn about the sacrifice that was made for you but the message is all the same. I am a sinner and I can never be good enough to get to heaven on my own (Romans 3:23). God sent His perfect son Jesus to be born of a virgin (John 3:16). Jesus died on the cross to save me from sin (Romans 5: 8). Jesus is alive today and rose from the grave on the third day defeating death (Romans

6:4). I can live with God in heaven for eternity! All I have to do is believe, trust and have faith in his birth, life, death, resurrection and His eternity! For many of us this is the easy part. The hard part is having the relationship with Him that He desires but that will come with growth and surrounding ourselves with Him.

If you have realized that you have not been living the life that God has called you to live and you are a born again Christian, maybe it is time for you to rededicate your life and start getting back on track. The best way to help accomplish this is to find a Christian you know and trust within your church. Tell this person that you are rededicating yourself to God. They do not have to know all the details, but ask this person to keep you lifted up in prayer, to help hold you accountable.

If you have realized that you have never know, God as your Lord and Savior but you want to, all you have to do is ask Him! You can say this prayer with me:

> *"Dear Lord, I now understand that I am a sinner. I can not get to heaven on my own. Lord I understand that you sent Jesus who was perfect with no sin to live on this earth. I know that He went to the cross to die for ME! That on the cross He took my sins upon Himself. Lord I know that Jesus died, but He rose again on the third day and lives today. Lord I want to be forgiven for my sins. I want to have a relationship with you. Lord, please come live in my heart and be my Lord and Savior. Thank you for saving me from my sins! Amen.*

Dear sister, if you just prayed this pray then hallelujah! The angels are rejoicing in heaven! This is just the first step. The Bible tells us that we need to let others know of our relationship with God. Many of us are not a good example, but there are those that are. Find a church to attend. Let them know that you have accepted Christ as your Lord and Savior and want to know how to have a relationship with Him. They will rejoice with you and lift you up. Don't be intimated by what you have done in the past; it is forgiven! Don't let it make you who you are today, but allow it to be an example of what you were and who you are not going to be.

# About the Author

MELINDA CULP HAS HER BACHELOR'S degree in nursing and is a pastor's wife. She conducts Bible studies for teens and women on a variety of subjects. She accepted Christ as a child, but during her teenage and college years, she stepped away from her walk with Christ and allowed the world to influence her decisions. As she renewed her commitment to Christ, spiritual and emotional healing occurred. He then set her on a path of dedicating her life to helping and encouraging women of all ages. She lives with her husband and two boys in Oklahoma.

Printed in the United States
By Bookmasters